A Note to Parents

Welcome to REAL KIDS READERS, a series of phonics-based books for children who are beginning to read. In the classroom, educators use phonics to teach children how to sound out unfamiliar words, providing a firm foundation for reading skills. At home, you can use REAL KIDS READERS to reinforce and build on that foundation, because the books follow the same basic phonic guidelines that children learn in school.

Of course the best way to help your child become a good reader is to make the experience fun—and REAL KIDS READERS do that, too. With their realistic story lines and lively characters, the books engage children's imaginations. With their clean design and sparkling photographs, they provide picture clues that help new readers decipher the text. The combination is sure to entertain young children and make them truly want to read.

REAL KIDS READERS have been developed at three distinct levels to make it easy for children to read at their own pace.

- LEVEL 1 is for children who are just beginning to read.
- LEVEL 2 is for children who can read with help.
- LEVEL 3 is for children who can read on their own.

A controlled vocabulary provides the framework at each level. Repetition, rhyme, and humor help increase word skills. Because children can understand the words and follow the stories, they quickly develop confidence. They go back to each book again and again, increasing their proficiency and sense of accomplishment, until they're ready to move on to the next level. The result is a rich and rewarding experience that will help them develop a lifelong love of reading.

For Allison
—S. H.

For my father, Sam, who always told
the best bedtime stories
—D. H.

Special thanks to Garnet Hill, Franconia, NH,
for providing clothing and bedding.

Produced by DWAI / Seventeenth Street Productions, Inc.
Reading Specialist: Virginia Grant Clammer

Library of Congress Cataloging-in-Publication Data

Hood, Susan.
    Time for bed? / Susan Hood ; photographs by Dorothy Handelman.
        p.   cm. — (Real kids readers. Level 2)
    Summary: A young girl tries various excuses to postpone bedtime, only to have difficulty
getting up in the morning.
    ISBN 0-7613-2069-5 (lib. bdg.). — ISBN 0-7613-2094-6 (pbk.)
    [1. Bedtime—Fiction. 2. Stories in rhyme.] I. Handelman, Dorothy, ill. II. Title. III. Series.
PZ8.3.H7577T1   1999
[E]—dc21   98-52513
                                                                                                        CIP
                                                                                                        AC

                        pbk: 10 9 8 7 6 5 4 3 2 1
                        lib: 10 9 8 7 6 5 4 3 2 1

Time for Bed?

By **Susan Hood**

Photographs by **Dorothy Handelman**

M

The Millbrook Press

Brookfield, Connecticut

You say it's late. It's time for bed.
But, Mom! I want to play instead.

Time for bed? I cannot go.
I have things to do, you know.
There is a song I want to play.
You say good night, but it's still day!

I have to study for a test.
I want to do my very best.
Okay, I'll put my books away.
Hey, look at this! I got an A!

.... Date ....

T WHAT YOU KNOW

Fill in each blank with one of the
animal groups that best describes the
sentence.

100% A

| amphibian | reptile | fish | bird | mammal |

1. These animals have wings, and most can fly. bird

2. These animals have fur or hair on their bodies. mammal

3. These animals have fins and scales and live in water. fish

4. These animals have feathers. bird

5. These animals have smooth, wet skin. amphibian

6. These animals drink milk from their mothers. mammal

7. These animals live in water when they are young but live on
   land when they get older. amphibians

8. These animals have dry, rough skin covered with scales. reptile

9. These animals have gills all their life to breathe. fish

10. Dinosaurs are reptiles that lived long ago.

I have a friend I need to call.
I *have* to know if she likes Paul.

I need a snack. I need a drink.
I need some time to sit and think.

Hey, look up there! Can you see stars?
And can you see the planet Mars?
How does the moon stay up in space?
Why does it have that silly face?

Okay, I'll put my nightgown on.
I need my bear. Where has he gone?

I have to brush my teeth and hair.
I have to pick out clothes to wear.

19

Here is my book. May I read, please?
I beg you, Mom. I'm on my knees.

What were you like, Mom, as a kid?
Please tell me all the things you did.
Did *you* like to go to bed?
Or did you want to play instead?

I need a hug. I need a kiss.
I need my blanket just like this.

I need to stretch. I need to yawn. . . .

Before I know it, it is dawn.
You say get up. Birds sing and cheep.
Get up now?

I need to sleep!

Phonic Guidelines

Use the following guidelines to help your child read the words in *Time for Bed?*

Short Vowels

When two consonants surround a vowel, the sound of the vowel is usually short. This means you pronounce *a* as in apple, *e* as in egg, *i* as in igloo, *o* as in octopus, and *u* as in umbrella. Short-vowel words in this story include: *bed, beg, but, can, did, get, got, has, hug, kid, mom, put, sit.*

Short-Vowel Words with Consonant Blends

When two or more different consonants are side by side, they usually blend to make a combined sound. In this story, short-vowel words with consonant blends include: *best, brush, drink, just, sing, snack, song, still, stretch, test.*

Double Consonants

When two identical consonants appear side by side, one of them is silent. In this story, double-consonants appear in the short-vowel words *kiss* and *tell*, and in the *all*-family words *all* and *call.*

R-Controlled Vowels

When a vowel is followed by the letter *r*, its sound is changed by the *r*. In this story, words with r-controlled vowels include: *birds, for, Mars, stars.*

Long Vowel and Silent E

If a word has a vowel and ends with an *e*, usually the vowel is long and the *e* is silent. Long vowels are pronounced the same way as their alphabet names. In this story, words with a long vowel and silent *e* include: *clothes, face, late, like, space, time.*

Double Vowels

When two vowels are side by side, usually the first vowel is long and the second vowel is silent. Double-vowel words in this story include: *day, may, need, play, please, read, say, see, sleep, stay, teeth.*

Diphthongs

Sometimes when two vowels (or a vowel and a consonant) are side by side, they combine to make a diphthong—a sound that is different from long or short vowel sounds. Diphthongs are: *au/aw, ew, oi/oy, ou/ow*. In this story, words with diphthongs include: *dawn, how, now, yawn.*

Consonant Digraphs

Sometimes when two different consonants are side by side, they make a digraph that represents a single new sound. Consonant digraphs are: *ch, sh, th, wh*. In this story, words with digraphs include: *cheep, that, there, things, think, this, what, where, why.*

Silent Consonants

Sometimes when two different consonants appear side by side, one of them is silent. In this story, words with silent consonants include: *knees, know, pick.*

Sight Words

Sight words are those words that a reader must learn to recognize immediately—by sight—instead of by sounding them out. They occur with high frequency in easy texts. Sight words not included in the above categories are: *a, an, and, as, at, do, does, friend, go, good, have, here, I, if, in, is, it, look, me, my, on, or, out, she, some, the, to, up, want, you.*